So Fucking Grateful!

A GRATITUDE JOURNAL
FOR BAD ASS WOMEN

Goldstar Journals

This fucking journal belongs to:

IF THAT ISN'T YOU STAY THE FUCK OUT!

Welcome to the shit show!

ONE GOOD
FUCKING THING
THAT HAPPENED
TODAY IS ....

DATE: _____

I AM SO FUCKING GRATEFUL FOR

SHIT I HAVE TO DO TODAY

- [ ]
- [ ]
- [ ]
- [ ]
- [ ]
- [ ]

ANOTHER KICK ASS DAY!

I'M SO GLAD I DIDN'T FUCKING DO THIS TODAY .....

DICKHEAD OF THE DAY

HOW MANY PEOPLE PISSED ME OFF TODAY?

(CIRCLE A CUPCAKE FOR EACH PERSON)

 ## NOTES & SHIT

I'M SO FUCKING PROUD OF MYSELF FOR THIS.....

IF TODAY SUCKED...LET THAT SHIT GO!

ONE GOOD
FUCKING THING
THAT HAPPENED
TODAY IS ....

DATE: _ _ _ _ _ _ _ _ _ _ _ _ _

I AM SO
FUCKING
GRATEFUL FOR

_____
_____
_____
_____

SHIT I HAVE
TO DO TODAY

- [ ] _____
- [ ] _____
- [ ] _____
- [ ] _____
- [ ] _____
- [ ] _____

ANOTHER KICK ASS DAY!

I'M SO GLAD I DIDN'T FUCKING DO THIS TODAY.....

ASSHOLE OF THE DAY

HOW MANY PEOPLE PISSED ME OFF TODAY?

(CIRCLE A CUPCAKE FOR EACH PERSON)

_____
_____
_____
_____

♥ NOTES & SHIT

_____

I'M SO FUCKING PROUD OF MYSELF FOR THIS.....

_____
_____
_____
_____
_____
_____
_____
_____

GET OUT THERE TOMORROW AND MAKE LIFE YOUR BITCH!

DATE: _ _ _ _ _ _ _ _ _ _ _ _ _ _

I AM SO
FUCKING
GRATEFUL FOR

_____
_____
_____
_____
_____

SHIT I HAVE
TO DO TODAY

- [ ] _____
- [ ] _____
- [ ] _____
- [ ] _____
- [ ] _____
- [ ] _____

ANOTHER KICK ASS DAY!

I'M SO GLAD I DIDN'T FUCKING DO THIS TODAY.....

JERK OF THE DAY

_____
_____
_____
_____

HOW MANY PEOPLE PISSED ME OFF TODAY?

(CIRCLE A CUPCAKE FOR EACH PERSON)

 # NOTES & SHIT

_____
_____
_____
_____
_____
_____
_____
_____
_____
_____

I'M SO FUCKING PROUD OF MYSELF FOR THIS.....

YOU'RE AMAZING. KEEP THAT SHIT UP!

ONE GOOD
FUCKING THING
THAT HAPPENED
TODAY IS ....

DATE: _____

I AM SO FUCKING GRATEFUL FOR

_____
_____
_____
_____
_____

SHIT I HAVE TO DO TODAY

☐ _____
☐ _____
☐ _____
☐ _____
☐ _____
☐ _____

ANOTHER KICK ASS DAY!

I'M SO GLAD I
DIDN'T FUCKING DO
THIS TODAY.....

JACKASS OF THE DAY

HOW MANY
PEOPLE PISSED
ME OFF TODAY?

(CIRCLE A CUPCAKE
FOR EACH PERSON)

_____
_____
_____
_____

♥ NOTES & SHIT

_____
_____
_____

I'M SO FUCKING PROUD OF
MYSELF FOR THIS.....

_____
_____
_____
_____
_____
_____
_____

FUCK THIS SHIT SHOW!

ONE GOOD
FUCKING THING
THAT HAPPENED
TODAY IS ....

DATE: _____

I AM SO
FUCKING
GRATEFUL FOR

_____

_____

_____

_____

_____

SHIT I HAVE
TO DO TODAY

- [ ] _____
- [ ] _____
- [ ] _____
- [ ] _____
- [ ] _____
- [ ] _____

ANOTHER KICK ASS DAY!

I'M SO GLAD I DIDN'T FUCKING DO THIS TODAY .....

DICKHEAD OF THE DAY

HOW MANY PEOPLE PISSED ME OFF TODAY?

(CIRCLE A CUPCAKE FOR EACH PERSON)

_____
_____
_____
_____

 NOTES & SHIT

_____
_____
_____
_____
_____
_____
_____
_____
_____
_____

I'M SO FUCKING PROUD OF MYSELF FOR THIS.....

IF TODAY SUCKED...LET THAT SHIT GO!

ONE GOOD
FUCKING THING
THAT HAPPENED
TODAY IS ....

DATE: _____

I AM SO
FUCKING
GRATEFUL FOR

_____

_____

_____

_____

_____

SHIT I HAVE
TO DO TODAY

- [ ] _____
- [ ] _____
- [ ] _____
- [ ] _____
- [ ] _____
- [ ] _____

ANOTHER KICK ASS DAY!

I'M SO GLAD I
DIDN'T FUCKING DO
THIS TODAY .....

BITCH OF THE DAY

HOW MANY
PEOPLE PISSED
ME OFF TODAY?

(CIRCLE A CUPCAKE
FOR EACH PERSON)

 NOTES & SHIT

I'M SO FUCKING PROUD OF
MYSELF FOR THIS.....

DON'T WORRY. BE FUCKING HAPPY AND SHIT!

DATE: _ _ _ _ _ _ _ _ _ _ _ _ _

I AM SO FUCKING GRATEFUL FOR

_____

_____

_____

_____

_____

SHIT I HAVE TO DO TODAY

- [ ] _____
- [ ] _____
- [ ] _____
- [ ] _____
- [ ] _____
- [ ] _____

ANOTHER KICK ASS DAY!

I'M SO GLAD I DIDN'T FUCKING DO THIS TODAY .....

ASSHOLE OF THE DAY

HOW MANY PEOPLE PISSED ME OFF TODAY?

(CIRCLE A CUPCAKE FOR EACH PERSON)

_____
_____
_____
_____

♥ NOTES & SHIT

_____
_____
_____

I'M SO FUCKING PROUD OF MYSELF FOR THIS.....

_____
_____
_____
_____
_____
_____
_____
_____

GET OUT THERE TOMORROW AND MAKE LIFE YOUR BITCH!

DATE: _____

I AM SO FUCKING GRATEFUL FOR

_____
_____
_____
_____
_____

SHIT I HAVE TO DO TODAY

☐ _____
☐ _____
☐ _____
☐ _____
☐ _____
☐ _____

ANOTHER KICK ASS DAY!

I'M SO GLAD I DIDN'T FUCKING DO THIS TODAY .....

JERK OF THE DAY

_____
_____
_____
_____

HOW MANY PEOPLE PISSED ME OFF TODAY?

(CIRCLE A CUPCAKE FOR EACH PERSON)

♥ *NOTES & SHIT*

_____
_____
_____
_____
_____
_____
_____
_____
_____
_____
_____

I'M SO FUCKING PROUD OF MYSELF FOR THIS.....

YOU'RE AMAZING. KEEP THAT SHIT UP!

ONE GOOD
FUCKING THING
THAT HAPPENED
TODAY IS ....

DATE: _____

I AM SO FUCKING GRATEFUL FOR

_____

_____

_____

_____

SHIT I HAVE TO DO TODAY

- [ ] _____
- [ ] _____
- [ ] _____
- [ ] _____
- [ ] _____
- [ ] _____

ANOTHER KICK ASS DAY!

I'M SO GLAD I DIDN'T FUCKING DO THIS TODAY .....

JACKASS OF THE DAY

HOW MANY PEOPLE PISSED ME OFF TODAY?

(CIRCLE A CUPCAKE FOR EACH PERSON)

_____
_____
_____
_____

 # NOTES & SHIT

_____
_____
_____

I'M SO FUCKING PROUD OF MYSELF FOR THIS.....

_____
_____
_____
_____
_____
_____
_____

FUCK THIS SHIT SHOW!

DATE: _____

I AM SO FUCKING GRATEFUL FOR

_____

_____

_____

_____

_____

SHIT I HAVE TO DO TODAY

☐ _____

☐ _____

☐ _____

☐ _____

☐ _____

☐ _____

ANOTHER KICK ASS DAY!

I'M SO GLAD I DIDN'T FUCKING DO THIS TODAY .....

BITCH OF THE DAY

_____

_____

_____

_____

HOW MANY PEOPLE PISSED ME OFF TODAY?

(CIRCLE A CUPCAKE FOR EACH PERSON)

♥ NOTES & SHIT

_____

_____

I'M SO FUCKING PROUD OF MYSELF FOR THIS.....

_____

_____

_____

_____

_____

_____

_____

_____

DON'T WORRY. BE FUCKING HAPPY AND SHIT!

DATE: _ _ _ _ _ _ _ _ _ _ _ _ _ _

I AM SO
FUCKING
GRATEFUL FOR

_____

_____

_____

_____

SHIT I HAVE
TO DO TODAY

- [ ] _____
- [ ] _____
- [ ] _____
- [ ] _____
- [ ] _____
- [ ] _____

ANOTHER KICK ASS DAY!

I'M SO GLAD I DIDN'T FUCKING DO THIS TODAY .....

DICKHEAD OF THE DAY

HOW MANY PEOPLE PISSED ME OFF TODAY?

(CIRCLE A CUPCAKE FOR EACH PERSON)

_____
_____
_____
_____

♥ NOTES & SHIT

_____
_____
_____
_____
_____
_____
_____
_____
_____
_____
_____

I'M SO FUCKING PROUD OF MYSELF FOR THIS.....

IF TODAY SUCKED...LET THAT SHIT GO!

DATE: _____

I AM SO FUCKING GRATEFUL FOR

_____

_____

_____

_____

SHIT I HAVE TO DO TODAY

- [ ] _____
- [ ] _____
- [ ] _____
- [ ] _____
- [ ] _____
- [ ] _____

ANOTHER KICK ASS DAY!

I'M SO GLAD I DIDN'T FUCKING DO THIS TODAY .....

BITCH OF THE DAY

_____
_____
_____
_____

HOW MANY PEOPLE PISSED ME OFF TODAY?

(CIRCLE A CUPCAKE FOR EACH PERSON)

♥ NOTES & SHIT

_____
_____

I'M SO FUCKING PROUD OF MYSELF FOR THIS.....

_____
_____
_____
_____
_____
_____
_____
_____

DON'T WORRY. BE FUCKING HAPPY AND SHIT!

DATE: _____

I AM SO FUCKING GRATEFUL FOR

_____

_____

_____

_____

_____

SHIT I HAVE TO DO TODAY

☐ _____

☐ _____

☐ _____

☐ _____

☐ _____

☐ _____

ANOTHER KICK ASS DAY!

I'M SO GLAD I DIDN'T FUCKING DO THIS TODAY.....

ASSHOLE OF THE DAY

HOW MANY PEOPLE PISSED ME OFF TODAY?

(CIRCLE A CUPCAKE FOR EACH PERSON)

_____
_____
_____
_____

♥ NOTES & SHIT

_____
_____
_____
_____
_____
_____
_____
_____
_____
_____

I'M SO FUCKING PROUD OF MYSELF FOR THIS.....

GET OUT THERE TOMORROW AND MAKE LIFE YOUR BITCH!

ONE GOOD
FUCKING THING
THAT HAPPENED
TODAY IS ....

DATE: _ _ _ _ _ _ _ _ _ _ _ _ _ _

I AM SO
FUCKING
GRATEFUL FOR

_____

_____

_____

_____

_____

SHIT I HAVE
TO DO TODAY

- [ ] _____
- [ ] _____
- [ ] _____
- [ ] _____
- [ ] _____
- [ ] _____

ANOTHER KICK ASS DAY!

I'M SO GLAD I DIDN'T FUCKING DO THIS TODAY .....

JERK OF THE DAY

_____
_____
_____
_____

HOW MANY PEOPLE PISSED ME OFF TODAY?

(CIRCLE A CUPCAKE FOR EACH PERSON)

♥ NOTES & SHIT

_____
_____
_____
_____
_____
_____
_____
_____
_____
_____

I'M SO FUCKING PROUD OF MYSELF FOR THIS.....

YOU'RE AMAZING. KEEP THAT SHIT UP!

ONE GOOD
FUCKING THING
THAT HAPPENED
TODAY IS ....

DATE: _____

I AM SO
FUCKING
GRATEFUL FOR

_____
_____
_____
_____
_____

SHIT I HAVE
TO DO TODAY

- [ ] _____
- [ ] _____
- [ ] _____
- [ ] _____
- [ ] _____
- [ ] _____

ANOTHER KICK ASS DAY!

I'M SO GLAD I DIDN'T FUCKING DO THIS TODAY .....

JACKASS OF THE DAY

_____
_____
_____
_____

HOW MANY PEOPLE PISSED ME OFF TODAY?

(CIRCLE A CUPCAKE FOR EACH PERSON)

♥ NOTES & SHIT

_____
_____
_____
_____
_____
_____
_____
_____
_____
_____
_____

FUCK THIS SHIT SHOW!

I'M SO FUCKING PROUD OF MYSELF FOR THIS.....

ONE GOOD
FUCKING THING
THAT HAPPENED
TODAY IS ....

DATE: _____

I AM SO
FUCKING
GRATEFUL FOR

_____

_____

_____

_____

SHIT I HAVE
TO DO TODAY

- [ ] _____
- [ ] _____
- [ ] _____
- [ ] _____
- [ ] _____
- [ ] _____

ANOTHER KICK ASS DAY!

I'M SO GLAD I DIDN'T FUCKING DO THIS TODAY .....

ASSHOLE OF THE DAY

_____
_____
_____
_____

HOW MANY PEOPLE PISSED ME OFF TODAY?

(CIRCLE A CUPCAKE FOR EACH PERSON)

♥ NOTES & SHIT

_____
_____
_____
_____
_____
_____
_____
_____
_____
_____

I'M SO FUCKING PROUD OF MYSELF FOR THIS.....

GET OUT THERE TOMORROW AND MAKE LIFE YOUR BITCH!

ONE GOOD
FUCKING THING
THAT HAPPENED
TODAY IS ....

DATE: _ _ _ _ _ _ _ _ _ _ _ _ _

I AM SO
FUCKING
GRATEFUL FOR

SHIT I HAVE
TO DO TODAY

- [ ] _____
- [ ] _____
- [ ] _____
- [ ] _____
- [ ] _____
- [ ] _____

ANOTHER KICK ASS DAY!

I'M SO GLAD I DIDN'T FUCKING DO THIS TODAY .....

DICKHEAD OF THE DAY

HOW MANY PEOPLE PISSED ME OFF TODAY?

(CIRCLE A CUPCAKE FOR EACH PERSON)

 NOTES & SHIT

I'M SO FUCKING PROUD OF MYSELF FOR THIS.....

IF TODAY SUCKED...LET THAT SHIT GO!

DATE: _____

I AM SO FUCKING GRATEFUL FOR

_____
_____
_____
_____

SHIT I HAVE TO DO TODAY

- [ ] _____
- [ ] _____
- [ ] _____
- [ ] _____
- [ ] _____
- [ ] _____

ANOTHER KICK ASS DAY!

I'M SO GLAD I DIDN'T FUCKING DO THIS TODAY .....

BITCH OF THE DAY

_____
_____
_____
_____

HOW MANY PEOPLE PISSED ME OFF TODAY?

(CIRCLE A CUPCAKE FOR EACH PERSON)

 NOTES & SHIT

_____
_____
_____
_____
_____
_____
_____
_____
_____
_____

I'M SO FUCKING PROUD OF MYSELF FOR THIS.....

DON'T WORRY. BE FUCKING HAPPY AND SHIT!

ONE GOOD
FUCKING THING
THAT HAPPENED
TODAY IS ....

DATE: _ _ _ _ _ _ _ _ _ _ _ _ _ _ _

I AM SO
FUCKING
GRATEFUL FOR

_____

_____

_____

_____

SHIT I HAVE
TO DO TODAY

- [ ] _____
- [ ] _____
- [ ] _____
- [ ] _____
- [ ] _____
- [ ] _____

ANOTHER KICK ASS DAY!

I'M SO GLAD I DIDN'T FUCKING DO THIS TODAY.....

ASSHOLE OF THE DAY

HOW MANY PEOPLE PISSED ME OFF TODAY?

(CIRCLE A CUPCAKE FOR EACH PERSON)

♥ NOTES & SHIT

I'M SO FUCKING PROUD OF MYSELF FOR THIS.....

GET OUT THERE TOMORROW AND MAKE LIFE YOUR BITCH!

ONE GOOD
FUCKING THING
THAT HAPPENED
TODAY IS ....

DATE: _____

I AM SO FUCKING GRATEFUL FOR

_____

_____

_____

_____

SHIT I HAVE TO DO TODAY

- [ ] _____
- [ ] _____
- [ ] _____
- [ ] _____
- [ ] _____
- [ ] _____

ANOTHER KICK ASS DAY!

I'M SO GLAD I DIDN'T FUCKING DO THIS TODAY .....

DICKHEAD OF THE DAY

HOW MANY PEOPLE PISSED ME OFF TODAY?

(CIRCLE A CUPCAKE FOR EACH PERSON)

_____
_____
_____
_____
_____

♥ NOTES & SHIT

I'M SO FUCKING PROUD OF MYSELF FOR THIS.....

IF TODAY SUCKED...LET THAT SHIT GO!

DATE: _____

I AM SO FUCKING GRATEFUL FOR

_____
_____
_____
_____

SHIT I HAVE TO DO TODAY

- [ ] _____
- [ ] _____
- [ ] _____
- [ ] _____
- [ ] _____
- [ ] _____

ANOTHER KICK ASS DAY!

I'M SO GLAD I DIDN'T FUCKING DO THIS TODAY .....

BITCH OF THE DAY

HOW MANY PEOPLE PISSED ME OFF TODAY?

(CIRCLE A CUPCAKE FOR EACH PERSON)

_____
_____
_____
_____

 NOTES & SHIT

_____
_____
_____

I'M SO FUCKING PROUD OF MYSELF FOR THIS.....

_____
_____
_____
_____
_____
_____
_____
_____

DON'T WORRY. BE FUCKING HAPPY AND SHIT!

ONE GOOD
FUCKING THING
THAT HAPPENED
TODAY IS ....

DATE: _____

I AM SO FUCKING GRATEFUL FOR

_____

_____

_____

_____

_____

SHIT I HAVE TO DO TODAY

- [ ] _____
- [ ] _____
- [ ] _____
- [ ] _____
- [ ] _____
- [ ] _____

ANOTHER KICK ASS DAY!

I'M SO GLAD I DIDN'T FUCKING DO THIS TODAY.....

ASSHOLE OF THE DAY

_____
_____
_____
_____

HOW MANY PEOPLE PISSED ME OFF TODAY?

(CIRCLE A CUPCAKE FOR EACH PERSON)

♥ **NOTES & SHIT**

_____
_____
_____
_____
_____
_____
_____
_____
_____
_____

I'M SO FUCKING PROUD OF MYSELF FOR THIS.....

GET OUT THERE TOMORROW AND MAKE LIFE YOUR BITCH!

ONE GOOD
FUCKING THING
THAT HAPPENED
TODAY IS ....

DATE: _____

I AM SO
FUCKING
GRATEFUL FOR

_____
_____
_____
_____

SHIT I HAVE
TO DO TODAY

☐ _____
☐ _____
☐ _____
☐ _____
☐ _____
☐ _____

ANOTHER KICK ASS DAY!

I'M SO GLAD I
DIDN'T FUCKING DO
THIS TODAY .....

JERK OF THE DAY

HOW MANY
PEOPLE PISSED
ME OFF TODAY?

(CIRCLE A CUPCAKE
FOR EACH PERSON)

♥ NOTES & SHIT

I'M SO FUCKING PROUD OF
MYSELF FOR THIS.....

YOU'RE AMAZING. KEEP THAT SHIT UP!

ONE GOOD
FUCKING THING
THAT HAPPENED
TODAY IS ....

DATE: _____

I AM SO FUCKING GRATEFUL FOR

_____
_____
_____
_____

SHIT I HAVE TO DO TODAY

- [ ] _____
- [ ] _____
- [ ] _____
- [ ] _____
- [ ] _____
- [ ] _____

ANOTHER KICK ASS DAY!

I'M SO GLAD I DIDN'T FUCKING DO THIS TODAY .....

JACKASS OF THE DAY

_____
_____
_____
_____

HOW MANY PEOPLE PISSED ME OFF TODAY?

(CIRCLE A CUPCAKE FOR EACH PERSON)

♥ **NOTES & SHIT**

_____
_____
_____
_____
_____
_____
_____
_____
_____
_____
_____

I'M SO FUCKING PROUD OF MYSELF FOR THIS.....

FUCK THIS SHIT SHOW!

DATE: _ _ _ _ _ _ _ _ _ _ _ _ _ _

I AM SO
FUCKING
GRATEFUL FOR

_____

_____

_____

_____

SHIT I HAVE
TO DO TODAY

☐ _____

☐ _____

☐ _____

☐ _____

☐ _____

☐ _____

ANOTHER KICK ASS DAY!

I'M SO GLAD I DIDN'T FUCKING DO THIS TODAY .....

BITCH OF THE DAY

_____
_____
_____
_____

HOW MANY PEOPLE PISSED ME OFF TODAY?

(CIRCLE A CUPCAKE FOR EACH PERSON)

♥ NOTES & SHIT

_____
_____
_____

I'M SO FUCKING PROUD OF MYSELF FOR THIS.....

_____
_____
_____
_____
_____
_____

DON'T WORRY. BE FUCKING HAPPY AND SHIT!

DATE: _____

I AM SO FUCKING GRATEFUL FOR

_____

_____

_____

_____

_____

SHIT I HAVE TO DO TODAY

- [ ] _____
- [ ] _____
- [ ] _____
- [ ] _____
- [ ] _____
- [ ] _____

ANOTHER KICK ASS DAY!

I'M SO GLAD I DIDN'T FUCKING DO THIS TODAY.....

DICKHEAD OF THE DAY

HOW MANY PEOPLE PISSED ME OFF TODAY?

(CIRCLE A CUPCAKE FOR EACH PERSON)

 NOTES & SHIT

I'M SO FUCKING PROUD OF MYSELF FOR THIS.....

IF TODAY SUCKED...LET THAT SHIT GO!

ONE GOOD
FUCKING THING
THAT HAPPENED
TODAY IS ....

I AM SO FUCKING GRATEFUL FOR

_____
_____
_____
_____

SHIT I HAVE TO DO TODAY

- [ ] _____
- [ ] _____
- [ ] _____
- [ ] _____
- [ ] _____
- [ ] _____

ANOTHER KICK ASS DAY!

I'M SO GLAD I DIDN'T FUCKING DO THIS TODAY.....

BITCH OF THE DAY

HOW MANY PEOPLE PISSED ME OFF TODAY?

(CIRCLE A CUPCAKE FOR EACH PERSON)

 NOTES & SHIT

I'M SO FUCKING PROUD OF MYSELF FOR THIS.....

DON'T WORRY. BE FUCKING HAPPY AND SHIT!

DATE: _____

I AM SO FUCKING GRATEFUL FOR

SHIT I HAVE TO DO TODAY

- [ ] _____
- [ ] _____
- [ ] _____
- [ ] _____
- [ ] _____
- [ ] _____

ANOTHER KICK ASS DAY!

I'M SO GLAD I DIDN'T FUCKING DO THIS TODAY .....

ASSHOLE OF THE DAY

HOW MANY PEOPLE PISSED ME OFF TODAY?

(CIRCLE A CUPCAKE FOR EACH PERSON)

_____
_____
_____
_____

♥ NOTES & SHIT

I'M SO FUCKING PROUD OF MYSELF FOR THIS.....

_____
_____
_____
_____
_____
_____
_____
_____
_____
_____

GET OUT THERE TOMORROW AND MAKE LIFE YOUR BITCH!

ONE GOOD
FUCKING THING
THAT HAPPENED
TODAY IS ....

DATE: _ _ _ _ _ _ _ _ _ _ _ _ _

I AM SO
FUCKING
GRATEFUL FOR

_____

_____

_____

_____

_____

SHIT I HAVE
TO DO TODAY

☐ _____

☐ _____

☐ _____

☐ _____

☐ _____

☐ _____

ANOTHER KICK ASS DAY!

I'M SO GLAD I DIDN'T FUCKING DO THIS TODAY .....

JERK OF THE DAY

_____
_____
_____
_____

HOW MANY PEOPLE PISSED ME OFF TODAY?

(CIRCLE A CUPCAKE FOR EACH PERSON)

♥ NOTES & SHIT

_____
_____

I'M SO FUCKING PROUD OF MYSELF FOR THIS.....

_____
_____
_____
_____
_____
_____
_____
_____
_____

YOU'RE AMAZING. KEEP THAT SHIT UP!

DATE: _____

I AM SO FUCKING GRATEFUL FOR

_____

_____

_____

_____

_____

SHIT I HAVE TO DO TODAY

☐ _____

☐ _____

☐ _____

☐ _____

☐ _____

☐ _____

ANOTHER KICK ASS DAY!

I'M SO GLAD I DIDN'T FUCKING DO THIS TODAY .....

JACKASS OF THE DAY

_____
_____
_____
_____
_____

HOW MANY PEOPLE PISSED ME OFF TODAY?

(CIRCLE A CUPCAKE FOR EACH PERSON)

♥ NOTES & SHIT

_____
_____
_____
_____
_____
_____
_____
_____
_____
_____
_____

I'M SO FUCKING PROUD OF MYSELF FOR THIS.....

FUCK THIS SHIT SHOW!

ONE GOOD
FUCKING THING
THAT HAPPENED
TODAY IS ....

DATE: _____

I AM SO FUCKING GRATEFUL FOR

_____
_____
_____
_____
_____

SHIT I HAVE TO DO TODAY

- [ ] _____
- [ ] _____
- [ ] _____
- [ ] _____
- [ ] _____
- [ ] _____

ANOTHER KICK ASS DAY!

I'M SO GLAD I DIDN'T FUCKING DO THIS TODAY .....

JERK OF THE DAY

HOW MANY PEOPLE PISSED ME OFF TODAY?

(CIRCLE A CUPCAKE FOR EACH PERSON)

_____
_____
_____
_____

♥ NOTES & SHIT

I'M SO FUCKING PROUD OF MYSELF FOR THIS.....

_____

YOU'RE AMAZING. KEEP THAT SHIT UP!

ONE GOOD
FUCKING THING
THAT HAPPENED
TODAY IS ....

DATE: _____

I AM SO
FUCKING
GRATEFUL FOR

_____
_____
_____
_____

SHIT I HAVE
TO DO TODAY

- [ ] _____
- [ ] _____
- [ ] _____
- [ ] _____
- [ ] _____
- [ ] _____

ANOTHER KICK ASS DAY!

I'M SO GLAD I DIDN'T FUCKING DO THIS TODAY.....

DICKHEAD OF THE DAY

HOW MANY PEOPLE PISSED ME OFF TODAY?

(CIRCLE A CUPCAKE FOR EACH PERSON)

_____
_____
_____
_____

♥ NOTES & SHIT

I'M SO FUCKING PROUD OF MYSELF FOR THIS.....

IF TODAY SUCKED...LET THAT SHIT GO!

ONE GOOD
FUCKING THING
THAT HAPPENED
TODAY IS ....

DATE: _____

I AM SO
FUCKING
GRATEFUL FOR

_____
_____
_____
_____

SHIT I HAVE
TO DO TODAY

- [ ] _____
- [ ] _____
- [ ] _____
- [ ] _____
- [ ] _____
- [ ] _____

ANOTHER KICK ASS DAY!

I'M SO GLAD I DIDN'T FUCKING DO THIS TODAY .....

BITCH OF THE DAY

HOW MANY PEOPLE PISSED ME OFF TODAY?

(CIRCLE A CUPCAKE FOR EACH PERSON)

♥ NOTES & SHIT

I'M SO FUCKING PROUD OF MYSELF FOR THIS.....

DON'T WORRY. BE FUCKING HAPPY AND SHIT!

ONE GOOD
FUCKING THING
THAT HAPPENED
TODAY IS ....

DATE: _____

I AM SO
FUCKING
GRATEFUL FOR

_____
_____
_____
_____

SHIT I HAVE
TO DO TODAY

- [ ] _____
- [ ] _____
- [ ] _____
- [ ] _____
- [ ] _____
- [ ] _____

ANOTHER KICK ASS DAY!

I'M SO GLAD I DIDN'T FUCKING DO THIS TODAY .....

ASSHOLE OF THE DAY

HOW MANY PEOPLE PISSED ME OFF TODAY?

(CIRCLE A CUPCAKE FOR EACH PERSON)

_____
_____
_____
_____

 NOTES & SHIT

_____
_____

I'M SO FUCKING PROUD OF MYSELF FOR THIS.....

_____
_____
_____
_____
_____
_____
_____

GET OUT THERE TOMORROW AND MAKE LIFE YOUR BITCH!

DATE: _____

I AM SO FUCKING GRATEFUL FOR

_____
_____
_____
_____
_____

SHIT I HAVE TO DO TODAY

- [ ] _____
- [ ] _____
- [ ] _____
- [ ] _____
- [ ] _____
- [ ] _____

ANOTHER KICK ASS DAY!

I'M SO GLAD I DIDN'T FUCKING DO THIS TODAY .....

JERK OF THE DAY

HOW MANY PEOPLE PISSED ME OFF TODAY?

(CIRCLE A CUPCAKE FOR EACH PERSON)

_____
_____
_____
_____

 # NOTES & SHIT

_____
_____
_____

I'M SO FUCKING PROUD OF MYSELF FOR THIS.....

_____
_____
_____
_____
_____
_____
_____

YOU'RE AMAZING. KEEP THAT SHIT UP!

DATE: _____

I AM SO FUCKING GRATEFUL FOR

_____

_____

_____

_____

SHIT I HAVE TO DO TODAY

- [ ] _____
- [ ] _____
- [ ] _____
- [ ] _____
- [ ] _____
- [ ] _____

ANOTHER KICK ASS DAY!

I'M SO GLAD I DIDN'T FUCKING DO THIS TODAY .....

JACKASS OF THE DAY

_____
_____
_____
_____

HOW MANY PEOPLE PISSED ME OFF TODAY?

(CIRCLE A CUPCAKE FOR EACH PERSON)

♥ NOTES & SHIT

_____
_____
_____
_____
_____
_____
_____
_____
_____
_____

FUCK THIS SHIT SHOW!

I'M SO FUCKING PROUD OF MYSELF FOR THIS.....

DATE: _____

I AM SO FUCKING GRATEFUL FOR

_____

_____

_____

_____

_____

SHIT I HAVE TO DO TODAY

- [ ] _____
- [ ] _____
- [ ] _____
- [ ] _____
- [ ] _____
- [ ] _____

ANOTHER KICK ASS DAY!

I'M SO GLAD I DIDN'T FUCKING DO THIS TODAY .....

BITCH OF THE DAY

HOW MANY PEOPLE PISSED ME OFF TODAY?

(CIRCLE A CUPCAKE FOR EACH PERSON)

_____
_____
_____
_____

 ## NOTES & SHIT

_____
_____

I'M SO FUCKING PROUD OF MYSELF FOR THIS.....

_____
_____
_____
_____
_____
_____
_____
_____
_____

DON'T WORRY. BE FUCKING HAPPY AND SHIT!

ONE GOOD
FUCKING THING
THAT HAPPENED
TODAY IS ....

DATE: _____

I AM SO FUCKING GRATEFUL FOR

_____
_____
_____
_____
_____

SHIT I HAVE TO DO TODAY

- [ ] _____
- [ ] _____
- [ ] _____
- [ ] _____
- [ ] _____
- [ ] _____

ANOTHER KICK ASS DAY!

I'M SO GLAD I DIDN'T FUCKING DO THIS TODAY.....

DICKHEAD OF THE DAY

HOW MANY PEOPLE PISSED ME OFF TODAY?

(CIRCLE A CUPCAKE FOR EACH PERSON)

_____
_____
_____
_____

 NOTES & SHIT

I'M SO FUCKING PROUD OF MYSELF FOR THIS.....

IF TODAY SUCKED...LET THAT SHIT GO!

DATE: _____

I AM SO FUCKING GRATEFUL FOR

_____
_____
_____
_____
_____

SHIT I HAVE TO DO TODAY

- ☐ _____
- ☐ _____
- ☐ _____
- ☐ _____
- ☐ _____
- ☐ _____

ANOTHER KICK ASS DAY!

I'M SO GLAD I DIDN'T FUCKING DO THIS TODAY .....

BITCH OF THE DAY

HOW MANY PEOPLE PISSED ME OFF TODAY?

(CIRCLE A CUPCAKE FOR EACH PERSON)

_____
_____
_____
_____

♥ NOTES & SHIT

_____
_____
_____
_____
_____
_____
_____
_____
_____
_____

I'M SO FUCKING PROUD OF MYSELF FOR THIS.....

DON'T WORRY. BE FUCKING HAPPY AND SHIT!

ONE GOOD
FUCKING THING
THAT HAPPENED
TODAY IS ....

DATE: _____

I AM SO FUCKING GRATEFUL FOR

SHIT I HAVE TO DO TODAY

- [ ]
- [ ]
- [ ]
- [ ]
- [ ]
- [ ]

ANOTHER KICK ASS DAY!

I'M SO GLAD I DIDN'T FUCKING DO THIS TODAY .....

ASSHOLE OF THE DAY

HOW MANY PEOPLE PISSED ME OFF TODAY?

(CIRCLE A CUPCAKE FOR EACH PERSON)

♥ NOTES & SHIT

_____
_____
_____

I'M SO FUCKING PROUD OF MYSELF FOR THIS .....

GET OUT THERE TOMORROW AND MAKE LIFE YOUR BITCH!

ONE GOOD
FUCKING THING
THAT HAPPENED
TODAY IS ....

DATE: _ _ _ _ _ _ _ _ _ _ _ _ _

I AM SO
FUCKING
GRATEFUL FOR

_____

_____

_____

_____

_____

SHIT I HAVE
TO DO TODAY

☐ _____

☐ _____

☐ _____

☐ _____

☐ _____

☐ _____

ANOTHER KICK ASS DAY!

I'M SO GLAD I DIDN'T FUCKING DO THIS TODAY .....

JERK OF THE DAY

———————————
———————————
———————————
———————————

HOW MANY PEOPLE PISSED ME OFF TODAY?

(CIRCLE A CUPCAKE FOR EACH PERSON)

♥ NOTES & SHIT

———————————
———————————
———————————
———————————
———————————
———————————
———————————
———————————
———————————
———————————

I'M SO FUCKING PROUD OF MYSELF FOR THIS.....

YOU'RE AMAZING. KEEP THAT SHIT UP!

DATE: _____

I AM SO FUCKING GRATEFUL FOR

_____
_____
_____
_____
_____

SHIT I HAVE TO DO TODAY

☐ _____
☐ _____
☐ _____
☐ _____
☐ _____
☐ _____

ANOTHER KICK ASS DAY!

I'M SO GLAD I DIDN'T FUCKING DO THIS TODAY .....

JACKASS OF THE DAY

HOW MANY PEOPLE PISSED ME OFF TODAY?

(CIRCLE A CUPCAKE FOR EACH PERSON)

 NOTES & SHIT

I'M SO FUCKING PROUD OF MYSELF FOR THIS.....

FUCK THIS SHIT SHOW!

ONE GOOD
FUCKING THING
THAT HAPPENED
TODAY IS ....

DATE: _____

I AM SO FUCKING GRATEFUL FOR

_____
_____
_____
_____

SHIT I HAVE TO DO TODAY

☐ _____
☐ _____
☐ _____
☐ _____
☐ _____
☐ _____

ANOTHER KICK ASS DAY!

I'M SO GLAD I DIDN'T FUCKING DO THIS TODAY.....

ASSHOLE OF THE DAY

HOW MANY PEOPLE PISSED ME OFF TODAY?

(CIRCLE A CUPCAKE FOR EACH PERSON)

_____
_____
_____
_____

♥ NOTES & SHIT

_____
_____
_____
_____
_____
_____
_____
_____
_____
_____
_____

I'M SO FUCKING PROUD OF MYSELF FOR THIS.....

GET OUT THERE TOMORROW AND MAKE LIFE YOUR BITCH!

ONE GOOD
FUCKING THING
THAT HAPPENED
TODAY IS ....

DATE: _ _ _ _ _ _ _ _ _ _ _ _ _

I AM SO
FUCKING
GRATEFUL FOR

_____
_____
_____
_____
_____

SHIT I HAVE
TO DO TODAY

- [ ] _____
- [ ] _____
- [ ] _____
- [ ] _____
- [ ] _____
- [ ] _____

ANOTHER KICK ASS DAY!

I'M SO GLAD I DIDN'T FUCKING DO THIS TODAY.....

DICKHEAD OF THE DAY

_____
_____
_____
_____

HOW MANY PEOPLE PISSED ME OFF TODAY?

(CIRCLE A CUPCAKE FOR EACH PERSON)

 NOTES & SHIT

_____
_____

I'M SO FUCKING PROUD OF MYSELF FOR THIS.....

_____
_____
_____
_____
_____
_____
_____
_____
_____

IF TODAY SUCKED...LET THAT SHIT GO!

DATE: _____

I AM SO FUCKING GRATEFUL FOR

_____

_____

_____

_____

SHIT I HAVE TO DO TODAY

☐ _____

☐ _____

☐ _____

☐ _____

☐ _____

☐ _____

ANOTHER KICK ASS DAY!

I'M SO GLAD I DIDN'T FUCKING DO THIS TODAY.....

BITCH OF THE DAY

_____
_____
_____
_____

HOW MANY PEOPLE PISSED ME OFF TODAY?

(CIRCLE A CUPCAKE FOR EACH PERSON)

♥ NOTES & SHIT

_____
_____
_____
_____
_____
_____
_____
_____
_____
_____

I'M SO FUCKING PROUD OF MYSELF FOR THIS.....

DON'T WORRY. BE FUCKING HAPPY AND SHIT!

DATE: _____

I AM SO FUCKING GRATEFUL FOR

SHIT I HAVE TO DO TODAY

- [ ] _____
- [ ] _____
- [ ] _____
- [ ] _____
- [ ] _____
- [ ] _____

ANOTHER KICK ASS DAY!

I'M SO GLAD I DIDN'T FUCKING DO THIS TODAY.....

ASSHOLE OF THE DAY

HOW MANY PEOPLE PISSED ME OFF TODAY?

(CIRCLE A CUPCAKE FOR EACH PERSON)

_____
_____
_____
_____

♥ NOTES & SHIT

I'M SO FUCKING PROUD OF MYSELF FOR THIS.....

GET OUT THERE TOMORROW AND MAKE LIFE YOUR BITCH!

DATE: _____

I AM SO FUCKING GRATEFUL FOR

_____
_____
_____
_____

SHIT I HAVE TO DO TODAY

☐ _____
☐ _____
☐ _____
☐ _____
☐ _____
☐ _____

ANOTHER KICK ASS DAY!

I'M SO GLAD I DIDN'T FUCKING DO THIS TODAY .....

JERK OF THE DAY

HOW MANY PEOPLE PISSED ME OFF TODAY?

(CIRCLE A CUPCAKE FOR EACH PERSON)

_____
_____
_____
_____
_____

♥ NOTES & SHIT

_____
_____

I'M SO FUCKING PROUD OF MYSELF FOR THIS.....

_____
_____
_____
_____
_____
_____
_____
_____
_____

YOU'RE AMAZING. KEEP THAT SHIT UP!

Made in the USA
Las Vegas, NV
14 November 2020